Stella Batts

Superstar

Stella Batts

Superstar

Book

8

Courtney Sheinmel

Illustrated by Jennifer A. Bell

For Jenn Daly, superstar

—Courtney

For V. S. and F.

—Jennifer

Text Copyright © 2015 Courtney Sheinmel
Illustrations Copyright © 2015 Jennifer A. Bell

Sleeping Bear Press™

2395 South Huron Parkway, Suite 200, Ann Arbor, MI 48104
www.sleepingbearpress.com
© Sleeping Bear Press

Red Hots® is a registered trademark of the Ferrara Pan Candy Company. Pop Rocks® is a registered trademark of Zeta Espacial S.A., Hot Tamales® is a trademark of Just Born, Inc., Bethlehem, PA, USA., Oreo® is a registered trademark of Kraft Foods.

Printed and bound in the United States.
10 9 8 7 6 5 4 3 2 1

Library of Congress Cataloging-in-Publication Data • Sheinmel, Courtney, author. • Stella Batts: superstar • written by Courtney Sheinmel ; illustrated by Jennifer A. Bell. • pages cm – (Stella Batts ; book 8) • Summary: Stella gets a chance to audition for her favorite television show when she meets a casting director who thinks she is perfect for the role, so she rehearses her lines until she know the part by heart, but the audition does not go as planned. • ISBN 978-1-58536-855-6 (hard cover) – ISBN 978-1-58536-856-3 (paperback) • [1. Auditions–Fiction. 2. Acting–Fiction. 3. Television–Production and direction–Fiction. 4. Family life–California–Fiction. 5. Schools–Fiction. 6. California–Fiction.] • I. Bell, Jennifer (Jennifer A.), 1977- illustrator. • II. Title. III. Title: Superstar. • PZ7.S54124Suj 2015 • [Fic]–dc23 • 2015003517

Table of Contents

Discovered..7

The Audition...21

No Promises 43

Script Changes by Stella Batts.......................61

The Opposite of Yippee...............................77

Another Script...87

I'm Sorry...105

Things Couldn't Get Much Worse...............117

Take Ten 133

Small Enough, Big Enough............................145

Wrap Party. 165

CHAPTER 1

Discovered

"Stella Stella bo bella banana fana fo fella me my mo mella . . . STELLA!"

Stella is my name, but the person singing was my sister, Penny. She was sitting across from me at Brody's Grill, the restaurant Mom and Dad had taken us to for dinner, even though it was a Monday, and we usually eat at home during the week. Mom and Dad said they didn't feel like cooking, and besides Brody's Grill is our favorite restaurant.

"*Ba ba ba ba ba ba ba.*"

That was my brother, Marco, singing nonsense.

"Penny." Now that was Mom. "Keep it down, please."

"It's Opposite Day!" Penny cried. "That means you want me to keep it up!"

"Penelope Jane," Mom said. "Inside voice. Now."

"Sometimes Mrs. Finkel tells Joshua to use an inside voice," I said.

Mrs. Finkel is my third-grade teacher, and Joshua is a kid in our class. He calls out a lot, and he's not just loud the way Penny is. He's mean, too.

"But I don't like to think about Joshua when we're not in school and I don't have to, because he's such a meanie," I added.

"That's not nice, Stel," Dad said.

"He's the one who's not nice," I said. "He's the biggest meanie in the whole third grade. And he's always getting in trouble because he breaks the Ground Rules, like using your inside voice. That's a rule in our class, you know."

"It's a Ground Rule at this restaurant, too," Mom said. "So all of the customers can enjoy their meals. All right, Pen?"

"Pa pa pa pa pa pa pa," Marco said.

"I think Marco's saying your name, Penny," Dad said.

"Use your inside voice, Marco!" Penny told him.

"Shhh, Penny," Mom said. "He's just a baby. He doesn't know any better. But you're five, and you do."

Penny folded her arms across her chest.

The waitress came over to our table. "Can

I bring you anything—coffee, tea?" she asked.

"Just the check whenever you get a chance," Dad said.

"I'm a little teapot," Penny began to sing.

"Penny," Mom said in a warning voice.

"What? I'm using my inside voice— my inside singing voice." And she started again. *"I'm a little teapot, shorty spout. Here is my handle, here is my spout. When I get all steamed up hear me shout. Tip me over and pour me out!"*

"Penelope Jane, that's enough," Mom said.

"Those weren't even the right words," I said.

"They were so," she said.

"They were not. It goes like this." I started to sing, *"I'm a little teapot—"*

"Stella, not you too," Mom said.

"I just need to teach her the right words,"
I said. "I'll be so quick. *I'm a little teapot,
SHORT and STOUT. Here is my handle, here
is my spout.*"

"All right," Mom said. "We've got it."

"Excuse me," a man said. "I'm sorry to
interrupt. I couldn't help but hear the concert
going on at your table."

"I'm so sorry we were bothering you," Mom told him. "What do you say, girls?"

"Sorry," I mumbled.

"I'm sorry, too," Penny said.

"Oh, no need to be sorry," the man said. "I rather enjoyed what I was hearing. I'm a casting director with Auditions Unlimited."

"Oh my goodness!" I said. "I've always wanted to meet a casting director."

"What's a casting director?" Penny asked.

"Someone who decides what people get to be in movies and TV and stuff like that," I told her.

"Movies and TV?" Penny asked. "Really?"

"Really," the man said. "Here, let me give your parents a card."

He handed it to Dad.

"I want to see," Penny said.

"Me too," I said. "I'll read it to you." I took

it and read out loud:

Hal Lewis, Director
Auditions Unlimited
101 Sanderson Drive
Somers, California

"All right, Stel," Mom said, reaching out for the card. "I'll take that now."

"Are we going to be famous?" Penny asked.

"I think we're getting a little ahead of ourselves here," Dad told her. He stuck his hand out toward Hal Lewis. "I'm David Batts. It's nice to meet you."

"Nice to meet you, too," Hal said. Then he shook hands with Mom, and then with me, and then with Penny. We all said our names. Well, except for Marco.

"Any relation to Joshua Lewis?" Mom asked.

Now I was thinking about Joshua again and it wasn't even my fault!

"Mom, lots of people have the same last name," I said, before Hal Lewis had a chance to answer. "It doesn't mean they're related. How would Joshua be related to a casting director?"

"And Joshua is already related to Bruce in my class," Penny said. "They're cousins."

"And they're both my nephews," Hal Lewis said. "Are you friends?"

"Stella's not friends with Joshua because he's a mean—" Penny started.

"Shh, Penny. She's just kidding," I said.

"Joshua and Stella go way back," Mom said.

"Naturally my nephew has charmed all the ladies," Hal said. "And speaking of these ladies, I'm looking for a young girl for a little scene in a TV show I'm casting. And I think your daughter—your older daughter—might just be perfect for it."

"Me? Really?" I asked.

"Yes, really," Hal said.

Oh my goodness! Oh my goodness! Oh my goodness!

"I'm so glad you didn't feel like cooking tonight!" I told Mom and Dad. "Could you imagine if we ate at home like usual and this never happened?"

"I wish it never happened," Penny mumbled.

"Should I go home and change my clothes?" I asked. Right then I was just wearing plain black leggings and a pink T-shirt, but I had better things at home. Like my jeans with the sparkles on the back pockets. Or my flower-girl dress from Aunt Laura's wedding.

"You don't have to do anything today," Hal Lewis said. "But if it's all right with your parents, you can come to my office tomorrow at twelve-thirty for an audition."

"Other kids are trying out for this part, too?" Mom asked.

"Yes," Hal Lewis said. "But we're in the last phase of auditions, so Stella would only have to come this one time."

"I don't know," Mom said. "Twelve-thirty is smack in the middle of the school day."

"Stella shouldn't be able to go, because she'd miss school," Penny said. "And also because if she gets to be on TV then it's not fair to me."

"It is too fair," I said. "Sisters don't always have to have the exact same things." Penny sat back in the booth and folded her arms across her chest. "Please, Mom? Please, Dad? Please?"

I asked. "I'll make up all my schoolwork. I'll do double the homework that night."

"I think Mom's just worried," Dad said.

"Worried?" I asked. "But why?"

"Because show business is a hard business," Mom told me. "I know it sounds like a lot of fun right now. But trust me. When I was young, I had a friend who was an actress."

"You did?" I asked. "That's so cool."

"It was sometimes," Mom said. "But most times it wasn't. My friend Dawn went on a lot of auditions, and usually she wouldn't get the part. The director would want someone taller, or shorter, or with darker hair. It made Dawn feel bad. I don't want that to happen to you."

"Excuse me," Hal said. "I just want to say—I can't make any promises here, but Stella has my vote. And it's a very good bit—in a show you might already know. It's called

Superstar Sam."

"*SUPERSTAR SAM*?!" I practically shouted, and then I remembered we were still in a restaurant and I was supposed to use my inside voice. "You know the show, Mom. It's my favorite. Sam is a gymnast, and she does all sorts of other cool things. That's how I knew what a casting director even was, because of the episode where Sam is going to be in a movie, but then she breaks her leg on the balance beam."

"Well, isn't this day full of coincidences," Hal said. "We'll be filming right here, too."

"In this restaurant?" I asked. "Don't you film at a studio?"

"Sometimes we film on location," Hal Lewis said. "I came here today to check this location out. And what good luck for me, because I got to meet you."

Good luck, as long as my parents agreed to let me audition. I clasped my hands together. "Please, Mom. Please, Dad. Please, pretty please, with a cherry on top? And sprinkles on top of that, and butterscotch icing, and another cherry?"

Mom looked at Dad, and Dad looked at Mom. And then they both looked over at Hal. "Okay," they said.

CHAPTER 2

The Audition

Mrs. Finkel clapped her hands at snack time, and I raced over to my friend Evie's desk.

Evie is my best friend, sort of. Another girl named Willa is my best friend in the whole entire world, but she moved to Pennsylvania. That's when Evie moved here from London. Now she's my best friend who lives in Somers.

Lucy, Talisa, and Arielle are more friends of mine. They also came over to Evie's desk. I couldn't wait to tell everyone my big news.

"You guys! I'm going to be on TV!"

"Are you serious?" Lucy asked.

"I'm very serious," I said. "My family was eating at Brody's Grill and this guy—this casting director—heard me singing, and he decided I was perfect."

"That's so cool," said Talisa.

"Hold on, you haven't heard the best part. The show I'm going to be on is *Superstar Sam*."

"No way!" Talisa said loudly.

"Talisa," Mrs. Finkel said in a warning voice. "Inside voice."

"Is that why you're all dressed up?" Arielle asked quietly, because that's the way she always talks.

That morning I'd put on a jean skirt that has ruffles at the bottom, and my pink T-shirt that has a bunch of rhinestones on it, that sort of look like real diamonds, plus sparkle tights.

"That's right," I told her.

"I knew it. You need to look good when you're going to be on TV."

"Well, I'm not going to be on today," I said. "I have to audition, but Hal Lewis said—Hal's the casting director, and he said—"

"Wait," Lucy cut in. "What would a casting director be doing here in Somers? Wouldn't he be in Hollywood? I don't think this is a for-real-life thing."

"It is too real life," I said. "You can ask Joshua. Hey, Joshua!"

"Stella Batts!" Mrs. Finkel said. "Inside voice, please."

Oops. I'd never gotten in trouble for not using my inside voice. "Sorry," I said.

"What, Smella?" Joshua asked.

Joshua always calls me Smella—that's

because he's such a meanie. But never mind that. I had an important question to ask him. "Your uncle Hal is a casting director, right?"

"Yeah," he said.

I turned back to Lucy. "I told you," I said.

"But Joshua sometimes lies," Lucy said.

"No, he doesn't," I said. Joshua can be mean, but he's not a liar. It's not the same thing. "Besides, why would he lie about this?"

Mrs. Finkel clapped her hands, which meant the talking part of snack time was over. I went back to my desk to eat my mini wafer cookies. But suddenly I didn't feel hungry. Not even for cookies. I don't like to eat when I'm nervous. What if Lucy was right? What if Hal Lewis had been lying? What if we got to his office building, and really there wasn't an audition at all?

Snack time ended. It was science time and we were learning about food groups. But it was hard to pay attention, because I was busy thinking about my audition. When Mrs. Finkel called on me, I said "Huh?" and she had to repeat the question again—is a tomato a vegetable or a fruit?

"Vegetable," I answered.

Mrs. Finkel shook her head. "It contains

seeds, so it's a fruit," she said. "Stella Batts, are you paying attention?"

I nodded while my cheeks turned Red Hots red.

Finally it was time for lunch. All the other kids had to line up to go to the cafeteria. But not me. I had to go to Mr. O'Neil's office. He's the principal. Mom was already at his office, waiting for me, and so was Penny. Mom and Dad had agreed she could also leave school early to see my audition. Penny had been complaining so much that everything wasn't fair, and they decided this would make it a little more fair.

"Break a leg, Stella," Principal O'Neil said.

"What?" How could the principal of my school say something like that?!

"It's just an expression," he explained. "It means good luck."

"Oh," I said. "Thank you."

In the car on the way, Mom reminded me that no matter what happened, I wasn't allowed to be sad.

"Remember Hal Lewis said I'm his first choice for the part."

"Just in case," she said. "Daddy and I will both be with you, and we don't want you to get too upset if things don't work out."

"Daddy's coming?" Penny asked.

"He's meeting us there," Mom said.

"Then who's staying with Marco?"

"We asked Mrs. Miller to stay with him."

"What if Marco wanted to see Stella's audition?" Penny asked. "Then it's not fair to make him stay with Mrs. Miller."

"He's just a baby," Mom said.

"Well, it's not fair to me that I don't get to audition too, because I'm not a baby anymore."

"No, you're not a baby anymore," Mom agreed. "So as a big girl and a good sister, I want you to be happy when nice things happen for Stella."

We drove down into a garage that went under the office building. Mom parked and we got out and walked back to the stairwell. We had to go to the third floor, because that's where Auditions Unlimited was. (There was an elevator too, but Mom said stairs are good exercise. Really it's because she doesn't like elevators.)

I was getting so excited that I raced up the stairs, all the way to the third floor, and pushed open the door right into a waiting room. There was a big sign over the reception desk that said: *Auditions Unlimited*.

That was proof that Lucy was wrong about it not being real. They wouldn't have a sign if it wasn't!

There were a bunch of other kids there already, with their parents. Most of them were sitting down, either on the couch or on folding chairs. But one of them was pacing back and forth across the room, and another was huddled in the corner with a woman who must've been her mom. The girl was reading from a piece of paper, and her mom was pointing to her own mouth and saying, "Smile! Smile!"

Superstar Sam wasn't anywhere to be seen.

"Name, please?" said the lady at the reception desk.

I was panting too hard from running up the stairs to answer right away.

"Excuse me?" the lady said. "Your name?"

The elevator dinged and Dad came out.

"Stella!" he said. "Did I miss anything?"

I shook my head.

"I'm trying to get her name," the reception lady said.

"Oh, Stella Batts," Dad said. "She has a twelve-thirty appointment."

"Right, I see her name here." She held out a piece of paper, same as the other kids had.

"Here, the script for the audition."

"Thanks," Dad said. He turned to me. "Where are Mom and Penny?"

I was still huffing and puffing, but at least I could talk a little now. "Walking up the stairs," I told him. "I ran up them."

Just then the stairwell door opened, and out they came. Everyone said hello. I looked

around for a place to sit, but all the seats were taken. "And your name is?" the receptionist asked.

"Penelope Jane Batts," Penny said. That's her real name. Penny is her nickname.

"She's not auditioning," I said.

"And it's not fair," Penny added.

"We have a cancellation," the receptionist said. "If Penelope wants to audition, she can."

"I do!" Penny said.

"But, Mom," I started. "She's only five. She's just auditioning to copy me!"

"No," Penny said. "Because it's my favorite show!"

"It's only your favorite show because you're copying me," I told her.

"Imitation is the sincerest form of flattery," Mom said.

That means it's supposed to be a

compliment when someone copies you, even though it's really just annoying.

"I'll take the script for my younger daughter, too," Mom told the receptionist.

"She's not such a good reader," I said.

"Shhh," Mom told me. "Penny, I'll help you."

I went to the corner of the room to read the paper myself. I read it so many times I knew it by heart forwards AND backwards. A few minutes later, a door behind the receptionist's desk opened, and a man with a clipboard called my name. "All right, darling, are you ready?" Dad asked.

He walked with me to the door. I thought he'd walk to the back room with me too, but the man shook his head. "We like to see the kids on their own."

I'd never been in a back room with a

stranger before, but Dad nodded, which meant I was allowed to go.

I followed the stranger down a hall and into another room, where three other people, two men and a woman, were sitting on folding chairs. Everybody told me their names—Edward, Joel, and Maureen.

"Where's Hal?" I asked.

"Hal Lewis?" Edward asked, and I nodded. "He had to take a personal day today, but he told us all about you."

"Oh cool," I said. "So now are we waiting for Superstar Sam?"

Maureen shook her head. "She won't be here today."

"So, Stella, whenever you're ready please read the words you have right there," Joel said.

"I thought I was supposed to memorize them."

"If you have them memorized, go ahead."

There weren't that many words on the paper and it wasn't hard to remember them. I clicked my heels together three times, for luck, took a deep breath, and said, "Just put ketchup on it. Ketchup is a vegetable." I paused and looked up at Maureen, Joel, and Edward. "Ketchup is made from tomatoes, right?" I asked.

"That's right," Joel said.

"Well, then ketchup can't be a vegetable because tomatoes are a kind of fruit. Maybe you can put that in the script."

"Don't worry about it," Edward said. "Can you say it the way it is in the script, one more time?"

"Sure," I said. I decided to mix things up a bit, and put on an English accent. Evie has an English accent since she's from London, and since we're such good friends, I've spent a lot of time listening to her. Maybe they wanted the character to sound international.

"Just put ketchup on it. Ketchup is a vegetable," I said. You can't tell reading it how it sounded, but trust me: it sounded practically like Evie's voice.

"Can you do it one more time?" Joel asked. "Without the accent. But a little louder

and with feeling."

"Pardon me?" I asked.

That's what Evie says whenever she doesn't understand something. It means: *What are you talking about?*

"A little emotion," he explained. "How do the words make you feel?"

Hmm. I'd never really thought about how ketchup made me feel. But I tried one more time in my regular voice, and then one more after then.

"Thank you, Stella," Maureen said. "We'll be in touch."

I went back to the waiting room. It was the perfect name for the room because first we waited for other kids to audition in front of Penny before her name was called. And then we waited for her to be done.

I picked up one of the magazines on the

coffee table and flipped through the pages. It had a lot of famous people in it, but not Superstar Sam. Next magazine. Next one. Next one. I hadn't ever heard of any of the people.

"Penny's taking a long time," I told Mom.

"She'll be out soon."

"I feel a little bad, like maybe she forgot the words, and she can't read them because she's only in kindergarten. She probably shouldn't have auditioned."

When Penny finally came back out, Joel was with her. "Mr. and Mrs. Batts?" he said. "Can I talk to you about your daughter?"

Mom and Dad stood up. All the grown-ups shook hands, and Joel said, "You have a talented daughter."

"Thank you," Dad said.

"We think two very talented daughters,"

Mom added.

"Oh yes, of course," Joel said. "And we'd like to make an offer to—"

I stood up too, and waited. I should shake his hand, right? Yes, that's what I'd do. A very grown-up thing, like having a job. Which is what I was about to have—a real job. The coolest job! Even cooler than owning a candy store!

"—your daughter Penelope," he finished.

What? WHAT?!

"What did you just say?" I asked.

"My name! He said my name!" Penny squealed. She jumped up and down. "Can you believe it? I'm going to be an actress! And a candy store owner, and a hotel owner, and a princess. But mostly an actress—and I don't even have to wait until I grow up!"

"Congratulations," Joel told her.

"But," I said. "But she's too young! Hal said so! I'm the exact right age to be Superstar Sam's friend. And Edward said he told you all about me. Didn't he also tell you that I was his first choice?"

"I'm sorry," Joel said. "But Hal doesn't get to make the final decision. When we met Penny, we decided to go in a different direction—Superstar Sam will be babysitting her."

"Stella, you promised you wouldn't be sad if you didn't get the part," Mom reminded me.

"It's nice that we got to keep the part in the family, right?" Dad added.

"Aren't you happy for me, Stella?" Penny asked.

"Sure she is," Mom said.

But I wasn't. I was so mad at her right then. It was worse than when she messed up my whole room. And worse than all the times she copied me.

If she hadn't auditioned, the part would probably be mine. It was the meanest thing she'd ever done to me.

I wished we'd never eaten at Brody's Grill for dinner after all.

CHAPTER 3

No Promises

I was sad, even if Mom said I couldn't be.

You can't help your feelings, after all. You just feel them. I was sad all that night, and the next morning, and the whole entire time I was at school.

I was still sad after school. Mom was waiting at the flagpole by the parking lot, since it was her day to drive us home. Here's who was riding in our car:

1. Mom
2. Me
3. Penny
4. Evie
5. Penny's friend Zoey

Penny was singing along with the radio. "You're such a good singer," Evie told her. "I'm not surprised you're going to be on TV."

"It was MY singing that Hal Lewis noticed," I said. "And she's not even going to sing when she's on TV."

"I'm a good actress, too," Penny said. "That's why I got the part."

"Mom, I have a question," I said. I wanted to change the subject. "Is Marco with Dad or Mrs. Miller?"

"Mrs. Miller," Mom said.

"Mom, I have a question, too," Penny said. "Bruce in my class said I'm going to get paid. Is that true?"

"It is indeed," Mom told her.

PAID?! I hadn't even thought of that. But of course she'd be paid, because being on TV is a job—the most fun job in the whole entire world—and people who have jobs get paid.

"I know what I want to get with my money," Penny said. She began to tick things off her fingers. "A piano, some baseball stuff, a bike, and French lessons."

"You're too young for French lessons," I told her. "I'm not even learning that yet."

"I'm teaching you," Evie reminded me. That was true—Evie had learned French at her old school in London, so she'd taught me some words. But still, I was in third grade and Penny was just in kindergarten.

"Besides I can do things even if you don't," Penny said.

I clicked my heels together three times, and wished the rule was: Older sisters get to do things before younger sisters do.

"I want a princess crown," Penny went on. "Because I'm going to be a princess when I grow up. A princess, and a writer, and own a candy store and a hotel, and be an actress!"

"Except you don't have to wait until you grow up to be an actress," Zoey said. "You already are one!"

We got to Zoey's house, and Zoey got out of the car. So did Penny, since she was going there for a playdate. I was having a playdate too, with Evie.

"So, girls," Mom said. "Since Mrs. Miller is with Marco, I was thinking we could go by the store for a while—you could play in the candy arcade, or help at the register."

"Ooh, I've always wanted to work a cash

register," Evie said.

"Does that sound good to you, Stel?" Mom asked.

"Please, Stella," Evie asked.

"All right," I said.

My favorite worker at Batts Confections, Stuart, saw us walking up to the store and he held the front door wide open for us. Mom headed downstairs to the office she shares with Dad, but Evie and I stayed upstairs with Stuart.

"So I hear your sister's going to be on TV," he said.

"Yeah," I said.

"Don't sound so glum, Stella," Stuart said.

"I can't help it," I told him. "The casting director wanted to give me the part, but then he wasn't there at the audition, and the other people wanted Penny."

"Sometimes people have different opinions about different things," Stuart said. "Look around this store—I bet if you asked everyone what their favorite candy was, you'd get a couple dozen different answers."

I looked around the store. And just then I had an idea. A really, REALLY good one.

"Have you ever worked a cash register before, Evie?" Stuart asked.

"No, I haven't—" Evie started.

"Wait a sec," I told her. "Come with me. I need you to help me with something."

Evie came to sit next to me on the bench by the fudge counter, and I told her my plan: We would sing, right here, right now. In front of all the Batts Confections customers. "Any one of them could be a casting director, like Hal Lewis was," I told her. "Like that woman with the blond hair by the Penny Candy Wall.

Or the man in line at the fudge counter."

"He doesn't look at all like a casting director to me."

"You never know what people's jobs are when you look at them and they're just strangers. And you never know if maybe they're going to want you to star in a TV show!"

"But I don't know how to sing," Evie said.

"Sure you do," I said. "Everyone knows how to sing. It's just like speaking except . . ." I paused. How do you explain to someone how to sing? "It's just like speaking, except you make your voice sound like a song, like *I'm a little teapot, la la la.*"

She sang, "*I'm a little teapot, la la la.*"

But she was right. She didn't sound so good. Not even with her cool accent. "Can you do anything else?" I asked. "Maybe tap dance or juggle?"

"I can wiggle my ears!" she said, and she pulled her hair back in her hands like in a ponytail, and she wiggled her ears! Without touching them! They moved all on their own!

"That's so cool! I'll sing, and you wiggle your ears. Then we'll be discovered together, and we can be famous together, which is way more fun."

"You're right. Should we start on three? Three, two, one—"

"No, wait. We need to find a different place, a better place, where more people can see us."

"Where, then?"

I looked around for a spot. The store was crowded, which made it hard for people to see me because I'm so short—I'm one of the shortest kids in my whole class. Evie's taller, but she's still only eight years old, which means she's shorter than most other people, too. "Come over here," I said.

"Stel, where are you headed?" Stuart asked.

"To the stairs," I told him.

"Don't go upstairs," Stuart said. "I want you to stay where I can see you. I can take you to the arcade in a few minutes, when I get someone to cover the register."

The arcade is what's up at the top of the stairs. "But we're not going all the way up," I told him. "We're just going to stand on the steps. You'll be able to watch us. In fact, you *should* watch us. We're going to perform!"

I grabbed Evie's hand and we headed to the stairs. Three steps up was just about the perfect height. Everyone could see us. "I just thought of something," Evie said. "We should rehearse first. Isn't that what people always do before they put on a show?"

I shook my head. "You don't have to

rehearse before you're discovered," I said. "Trust me, this just happened to me."

"All right. So when do we start?"

"I think, one . . . two . . . three . . . NOW!"

"*I'm a little teapot*," I sang, while Evie held back her hair and wiggled her ears. "*Short and—*"

"Excuse me," a lady said, coming up the stairs.

Oh great! That was fast! We were about to be discovered already!

"Yes?" I said.

"So, can you step aside so I can get past?"

"Yeah, sure," I said.

I stepped down so I was standing on a lower step, and the lady headed up. "Should we start again?" Evie asked.

"Yeah, but we should probably find a different space. Maybe we don't need to be

higher up. The last time I was discovered I was sitting down."

"How about over there?" Evie asked. She pointed to the popcorn machine next to the candy circus. "That's always a crowded space, so more people will hear us."

"That's a great idea!" I told her.

We jumped down the last of the stairs and crossed the room to the candy circus. Stuart was watching us the whole time—keeping an eye on us, like he'd promised Mom. "Okay," I said. "One . . . two . . . three . . . NOW!"

"*I'm a little teapot*," I sang. "*Short and stout.*" I made it through the whole song. Evie wiggled her ears and did the hand motions for the song, too. It was great—we hadn't even planned it. It just happened naturally. There were at least ten people by the popcorn machine, and they all watched us. But when we were done, no one came up to talk or give us any business cards.

"Now what?" asked Evie.

I shrugged. Above the front door, the bell jingled as another customer came in. "We might have to perform a few more times," I said. "Because more people are coming into the store, and you never know who is going to be a casting director."

"Should we start again right now?"

"Stella! Evie!" Dad called. "Come on over here, please."

He was standing by Stuart at the register.

"Stuart told me there's a little show going on over there," he said when we reached him.

"Yes, there is. We're trying to be discovered."

"I see," Dad said.

"But so far, I don't think any of the

customers are casting directors. Hey, Dad, you have Hal Lewis's card, right? Can you call him, and invite him to the store so he can see our show?"

"I'm sure he's busy right now, Stel," Dad said. "And besides, the show he was working on was already cast."

"But maybe if he saw me sing again, he'd remember that he really wants me to be in it."

"And me too," Evie said.

"Right, Evie too," I said. "She can wiggle her ears."

"That's very impressive, Evie," Dad said. He turned to me. "Show business is a tough business, like Mom said. But different people have different talents. Even if you're not going to be on TV, there are a lot of things that make you special."

"Like what?"

"Like you're a very talented writer."

"I want to do both," I said. "It's not too many things."

"No, it's not," Dad agreed.

"So can we try and be discovered some more?"

"Tell you what," Dad said. "Why don't we go up to the candy arcade for a bit?"

"You're trying to change the subject," I told him. "That's what you always do to distract Penny. But I really want to be in a show, and meet Superstar Sam, and Evie does, too."

"How about a compromise?" Dad said. "I'll call Hal and see if we can get an extra pass to the filming on Friday. That way you can have Evie with you—not to audition, but to watch. Would you like that, Evie?"

"I've never seen the show, but it sounds

like fun. It's always fun to be with Stella."

"No promises," Dad said. "But I'll try. What do you say, Stella? You'd like Evie there, right?" I nodded, because I would like Evie there. I'd like her there even more if I was going to be in the show.

CHAPTER 4

Script Changes by Stella Batts

The next day, Penny and I got dropped off at home after school. We went to the kitchen to have a snack. Mom sliced a banana and split a Batts Bar, which is the best kind of chocolate bar in the whole entire world.

"How was school?" Mom asked us.

"I signed my first autographs!" Penny said.

"What?" I asked.

"Autographs," she repeated. "When you

write your name on a piece of paper. Except it's not the same as writing your name on the top of your homework, or on a picture you drew so you know which one is yours. Someone else wants you to write it out so they can have it."

"I know what an autograph is," I said. "I just don't know why you're signing them."

"Because I'm famous."

"No, you're not."

"I am so," Penny said. "That's what happens when you're on TV. Everyone wants your autograph so they can keep it forever, because you're so special."

"Penny," Mom started. "You know Daddy and I agree you're very special."

"I know," Penny said.

"But being on TV is just an experience you're having. It's not a characteristic that's making you more special. The great things about you are still great even if you're not on TV. Do you understand?"

"Yeah, I do," Penny said.

But she was wrong, and so was Mom. And the proof is what Mom told Penny next: "You got an e-mail today."

Penny never got e-mails. She bounced up and down in her seat. "An e-mail for me? Really?"

"Settle down and I'll show you," Mom said. "There are some changes to the script."

"But I already memorized my other script."

"I know," Mom said. "But that's the way it works. They make changes to the script and you just have to roll with it. Shall we practice?"

"The show isn't until Friday," I reminded everyone.

"Dawn always felt better when she'd practiced more," Mom said. "I thought we could read the new script today and again tomorrow, so your sister is all set for Friday."

"Goody!" said Penny.

"Only if it's Opposite Day," I muttered.

"Stella, we had a deal about this," Mom said. "And the deal was, you couldn't be upset if you didn't get the part."

The deal didn't include what would happen if *Penny* got the part.

"If you can't be a supportive sister, then

you should go to your room to do your homework," Mom continued.

"I didn't finish my snack yet," I said.

"I did!" Penny said. She wiped her hands on a napkin and stood up. "I'm ready to practice my lines!"

Mom had printed out the e-mail with the script changes and she brought it over to the table.

"There are three characters in your scene," Mom said. "We'll read it together. You can read the part of Sam if you want, Stella."

I shook my head. "I still have some banana pieces to finish."

"Suit yourself. Look here, Pen. You have three lines now." Mom traced the words on the page with her finger so Penny could follow along. "The waiter comes over to take your order, and Sam says you need to add a vegetable. You say, 'Ketchup is made of tomatoes, right?' Then Sam says, 'I think it is.' Then the waiter says, 'Tomatoes are a fruit, not a vegetable.' "

"That was MY idea!" I said. "I told Maureen and Joel and Edward about that."

"Isn't that something, Stella!" Mom said.

"Then what do I say?" Penny asked.

Mom turned back to her. "Then you pick up the bottle and say, 'I can do it myself.' "

"That's true," Penny said. "I *could* do it myself."

"I'm sure you could," Mom said. "But look here, when your character squeezes the bottle, the ketchup gets splattered over everything. You have one last line and that's 'Uh-oh.' "

"That's so funny," Penny said.

"Are you ready to practice?" Mom asked.

"Yuppers!"

I put a slice of banana in my mouth and chewed slowly as they practiced. Penny stumbled over her lines. "Let's do it again," Mom said.

"Yeah, with more feeling this time," I added.

"What does that mean?" Penny asked.

"It means think about how the words make you feel and say them like that," I explained.

"That's an excellent piece of advice," Mom said. "If you spilled the ketchup, how would you say 'Uh-oh'?"

"Like this," Penny said. "UH-OH!!!!!!!!"

"Wahhhh!" called Marco.

"I think maybe a little bit less feeling than that," Mom said. "Let me go check on your brother."

"But I didn't mean to wake him," Penny said. "And we still have to practice."

"When one of my kids is crying, that's the kid I have to take care of first," Mom said. "It's a Mom Rule. But maybe Stella will help you, if you ask nicely."

"But, Mom," I started.

But Mom was out the door.

"Pretty please with a cherry on top, and whipped cream, and sprinkles, and Penny Candy, and Marco's Minis, and Stella's Fudge, will you help me?" Penny asked.

She slid the script over to me and I looked at it. I couldn't help myself. This is what I saw:

WAITER

Have you decided what to order, kids?

SAM

Almost. Quinn here just needs to decide on a vegetable. Broccoli or carrots?

QUINN

Ketchup is made of tomatoes, right?

SAM

I think it is.

WAITER

Tomatoes are a fruit, not a vegetable.

SAM picks up the bottle to examine the label. QUINN grabs it from her.

QUINN

I can do it myself!

Ketchup is accidentally squeezed out and ends up all over the table.

QUINN

Uh-oh.

I finished reading the scene.

It was pretty good, better than the last version. There are so many ways to write a scene. And suddenly I had another idea—even better than the one about getting discovered in Batts Confections.

"Here, Penny," I said. "I want you to rehearse it this way. Instead of you saying 'Uh-oh,' *I'll* say it."

"Why? In the script Quinn is supposed to say it—and that's me."

"I'm going to rewrite it," I told her. "You heard Mom. That's a thing that happens a lot to scripts. I'm a writer so I'll rewrite it and make a part for me. What do you think?"

"Then we could both be on TV!" Penny said.

"I just have to decide what my character's name will be. How about . . . how about . . ."

"How about Penelope?"

"Sure," I said. "I'll be Penelope. Let me get some paper."

But before I could get any paper, the

phone rang. I looked at the caller ID. "Lewis, Harold," it said. That had to be Hal Lewis. What perfect timing that he was calling right then at that very moment.

"Let the machine get it!" Mom called. Which meant she was still busy with Marco.

But I answered instead. "Hello? Hal Lewis? This is Stella Batts."

"Hello, Stella Batts," he said. "It's good to talk to you. Is your dad around? He left me a message the other day."

"He's not home."

"Can I speak to your mom then?"

"She's busy taking care of my baby brother," I told

him. "But you can talk to me because I know why my dad was calling. He had a question for you. And Penny and I just thought of another question for you. So we have two questions."

"Let's hear 'em," Hal Lewis said.

"Okay, my first question is, is it possible to get another pass to the filming so my friend Evie can come?"

"Oh, Stella, I'm sorry," Hal Lewis said. "We are filled to capacity. I hope you understand."

"I understand," I said.

Actually, it didn't matter as long as Hal Lewis said yes to the next question. If I was an actress on the show like Penny, I wouldn't need a pass, and Evie could take mine.

"The next question is the more important one anyway," I told him. "You know how

Penny got changes to the script?"

"I do know," Hal Lewis said.

"Well, did you know some of my ideas are actually in it?"

"I didn't know that," he said. "Congratulations."

"Thanks, and I had a really good idea to write another character into the scene. Sam could be babysitting Quinn with a friend and—"

"Stella, I'm going to stop you right there, because I'm sure you're an excellent writer."

"Thank you," I said.

"But the truth is, we don't need another writer on this script. Everyone is happy about how it turned out, and we're just going to proceed with it as is, with Penny in the scene. But I'll see you at the filming, all right?"

But it wasn't all right. It was all wrong.

And I didn't answer his question because I didn't want to lie.

"Gotta go," I said. "Bye." And I hung up the phone.

CHAPTER 5

The Opposite of Yippee

"I'm not going to watch the show being filmed," I said.

"Oh, Stel," Mom said. She'd come back into the kitchen after Marco had finally fallen asleep. "Don't cut off your nose to spite your face."

"Cut off your nose to Spiderface?" Penny asked. "Who's Spiderface?"

"No, 'to spite her face,'" Mom said, more slowly this time.

"Stella wouldn't ever do that," Penny said. "She'd look so weird, like an alien. And then how would she even breathe?"

I put my hand to my nose to make sure it was still there. Even though of course I knew it was still there. Still, you can never be too careful. "Penny's right," I said. "I'd never cut my nose off!"

"It's just an expression," Mom said. "It means don't make a situation worse just because you're upset about it. In this case, you shouldn't throw away this great opportunity to watch your sister and meet your favorite star just because things aren't working out exactly the way you want them to."

I shook my head. It wasn't such a good opportunity. It was just a sad opportunity.

"If Stella's not going, then we have an extra pass, right?" Penny asked.

"Stella's going," Mom said.

"It's not a Ground Rule for me to go is it?" I asked.

"No, of course not," Mom said. "But I have a feeling you'll change your mind. Penny, tell your sister that you want her to change her mind."

"I want you to change your mind," Penny said. She paused, and looked back up at Mom. "But if she doesn't change her mind, then Evie can go, right? She wants to go. Stella said."

"I'm not going to change my mind," I said.

"Goody!" Penny said. "I mean not goody that Stella won't come, but goody that Evie can. Can I call her now? What's her number?"

"*I'll* call her," I said.

After all, she was my best friend. That's why I knew her number by heart. I still had the phone by me, and I picked it back up.

"Let me have it!" Penny said.

"No, I want to talk first."

"But it's my invitation," Penny said.

"She might not even want to go," I said.

"But you said she did," Penny said.

"That was back when she thought I'd be there, too," I said. I dialed Evie's number. "It's ringing," I reported.

"Hello?" Mr. King said.

"Hi, Mr. King," I started. But then Penny grabbed the phone away. "Hold on, wait! I was talking!"

"Hello? Hello?" I heard Mr. King say on the other line, but now Penny had the receiver in both of her hands, holding on tight so I couldn't take it back and answer him.

"Girls!" Mom said.

"It's not my fault," I said, at the same time that Penny said, "It's not fair!"

Mom took the phone away from both of us. "Hugh, it's Elaine Batts," she said. "We're having a little battle over here about who gets to speak to Evie first." Mom paused and she smiled, which meant Mr. King had said something funny. "Yes, your daughter certainly is popular in our house. But thanks, that's a great idea."

"What's a great idea?" Penny broke in.

"Shh," Mom said. But I was wondering the same thing. Mom lowered the phone from her ear and turned to Penny and me. "Mr. King is going to get Evie now, and I'll put her on speakerphone."

"That is a great idea!" Penny said.

"Yes," Mom said. "But you girls still need to take turns speaking, so Stella, you can go first."

"But—" Penny said.

Mom cut her off. "It *is* fair, Penny."

"How'd you know what I was going to say?"

"Because I'm your mom, and I pay a lot of attention to you."

"Hello?"

"Evie!" Penny and I cried.

"Hi, Stella! Hi, Penny!"

"And my mom too," Penny said.

"Hi, Mrs. Batts, how are you?"

"I'm fine, thank you, Evie. How are you?"

"I'm good, I was just practicing my gymnastics to be like Superstar Sam."

"You see," Penny said.

"She doesn't even know the show, really," I told Penny. "She was just practicing because I told her about it. But actually, Evie, there's been a change of plans, and I'm not going to the filming after all."

"What? Why?"

"It's just something I decided," I said. "Since I'll be free after school on Friday, I thought maybe you could come over. We could watch a movie, or maybe go to the store and help sell things again, or we could—"

"Or you could take Stella's place and watch me be famous and meet Superstar Sam!" Penny cut in.

"But she doesn't even watch the show," I reminded Penny. "So she doesn't care about meeting Superstar Sam."

"Actually my dad showed me on his computer, and I quite like it," Evie said.

"So does that mean you will come?" Penny asked.

"Sure," Evie said.

"You don't have to just to be nice," I told her.

"I'm not saying yes just to be nice," Evie said. "I really want to."

"Yippee!" Penny said.

I don't know what the opposite of *Yippee*
is, but that's what I was thinking right then.

CHAPTER 6

Another Script

A True Story of What Happened
in the Lunchroom
Written by: Stella Batts

*It is lunchtime at Somers Elementary School.
All the kids are sitting at tables. STELLA (that's
me, obviously) gets to the table and all the good
seats are already taken. The only empty seat is
next to JOSHUA.*

EVIE

What took you so long, Stella?

STELLA

I had to buy lunch today and then I was afraid of spilling the juice so I walked extra slow.

LUCY

See, Evie, that's something Superstar Sam would be really great at, because she's good at balancing. I'm pretty good at balancing too, but I bring my juice in a thermos, so it doesn't spill. And also I bring a sandwich, so I don't have to eat—what is that you have to eat, Stella?

STELLA

It's turkey with gravy.

JOSHUA

It doesn't look like it.

ARIELLE

It might taste good though.

TALISA

Hey, I have a joke. Knock knock.

EVERYONE

Who's there?

TALISA

Gross.

EVERYONE

Gross who?

TALISA

Gross, it's the school lunch!

STELLA

That's not a real knock-knock, you know.

TALISA

I know. I made it up. You're allowed to make up knock-knock jokes.

JOSHUA

Why didn't you bring your lunch, Smella?

EVIE

She forgot it, and when she remembered it was too late to turn back around, so my dad gave her pounds to buy one.

LUCY

Pounds?

EVIE

Oops, I mean dollars.

TALISA

I wish it was English money! I want to see it!

EVIE

I'll bring some in.

TALISA

Plus the autographs from Superstar Sam!

STELLA

What autographs?

LUCY

Evie is going to see *Superstar Sam* being made—

JOSHUA

I'm going too, and Smella's going.

EVIE

No, she's not going anymore.

JOSHUA

Why not?

STELLA

I decided I didn't want to go, so Evie took my place.

TALISA

Evie's so lucky! I wish I could go!

JOSHUA

How come you don't want to go, Smella?

LUCY

It's none of your beeswax, Joshua. And anyway, it's okay because Evie's going to bring us autographs from Superstar Sam! You have to pay lots of attention and report back on everything you learn about her, too.

EVIE

I will!

STELLA looks down at her plate. She picks up her fork and takes a bite of her food. It tastes so bad that she needs to gulp down almost all of her orange juice.

STELLA

Can I borrow someone's napkin?

EVIE

Sure, take mine.

STELLA opens the napkin up and uses it to cover her whole entire plate of turkey.

LUCY

Why'd you do that?

STELLA

It tasted bad, and I didn't want to look at it
anymore.

EVIE

You don't need to give it back.

STELLA

What?

EVIE

You said you were going to borrow the napkin,
but you can keep it!

STELLA

Thanks.

STELLA'S *stomach rumbles.*

JOSHUA
I heard that!

LUCY
Your face is turning red.

STELLA
It's not my fault. I didn't have snack, and now I'm not getting lunch except for juice.

ARIELLE
You can have some of my apple slices.

EVIE
You can have the other half of my sandwich. I'm too excited to eat!

LUCY

Yes, tell us more!

EVIE

Well, I don't know very much yet, but I've been practicing my cartwheels.

STELLA

You don't get to be on the show, you know.

EVIE

I know, but I'm still inspired. Maybe I'll be a gymnast, too.

LUCY

I want to be a gymnast. I've got great balance, like I said.

TALISA

And I'm really good at a roundoff.

EVIE

What's a roundoff?

TALISA

It's a type of cartwheel, but way better. If you want, I can teach you.

EVIE

Thanks!

ARIELLE

You didn't like the apples, Stella?

STELLA

They were fine. I just wasn't so hungry after all.

Brrrring brrring brrring
(That was the bell, which meant lunch was
over and it was time for recess.)
Everyone stands up.

MISS LINKA

All right, kids. Let's be organized about this.
Lunch boxes should be put on the windowsill.
Or if you have a tray, carry it to the conveyor
belt.

TALISA

C'mon, Evie! I'll teach you right now!

Kids dropped their lunch boxes on the
windowsill and ran toward the playground.
Except you're not supposed to run, so really
they were walking super fast so it was almost
like running.

STELLA picked up her tray and walked to the back of the room, toward the conveyor belt. Most of the orange juice was all drunk up, so she didn't have to walk as slowly as before.

Except then JOSHUA bumped into her, and the tray slipped from her hands and smashed down on the ground. Crash! The plate with the turkey flipped over, and the gravy made a puddle on the floor.

JOSHUA

Watch where you're going, Smella.

STELLA

You're the one who bumped into me!

MISS LINKA

Can you get some napkins, Joshua?

JOSHUA

But it wasn't my fault!

MISS LINKA

Fault doesn't matter. We just need to get it
cleaned up. Come on.

JOSHUA gets a stack of napkins.

JOSHUA

I know why you're not going to the show.

STELLA

No, you don't, because I didn't tell you, and you can't read my mind.

JOSHUA

I can so. It's because you didn't get the part and you're jealous of Penny. My uncle told me so.

STELLA is quiet for a few seconds. MISS LINKA hands her another napkin.

STELLA

You're making that up, Joshua, but I'll tell you the real reason. Because you're going to be there and I don't like being near you! Why do you even sit with us at lunch when you're not even our friend?

JOSHUA

I was going to help you clean up, but now I'm not. You're on your own, Spilla.

STELLA

That doesn't even rhyme with Stella.

JOSHUA

Fine, you're still Smella, with the stinky turkey smell all over you.

THE END

(Sorry, this play did not have a happy ending.)

I'm Sorry

Things went from bad to worse when I got home. I made the mistake of telling Mom that I'd written a script of what had happened in the lunchroom. "May I see it?" Mom asked.

I opened my backpack, pulled out my notebook, and handed it over.

Usually when Mom reads things I've written, she smiles and says, "Stella! I'm so proud of your writing!"

But this time Mom was NOT smiling,

and when she opened up her mouth to speak, this is what she said: "I think we need to have a little talk, Stel."

"You didn't like it," I said.

"Stella, come sit," Mom said. She sat down on my bed, and patted the space on the mattress right next to her. There was a lump in my throat like a gobstopper, and my eyes burned like I'd eaten a handful of Hot Tamales. I sat down next to Mom, and she went on. "I think your script was just fine. In fact, I think it was very well done."

"So why do we need to talk?" I asked.

"Because when I read it, I felt really sad for one of the characters," she said.

"Me?" I asked.

"Well, yes, Stel. I'm always sad when you're sad," Mom said. "But I was thinking about another character—I was thinking about Joshua."

Did she just say JOSHUA?!!!

How could she feel bad for him? "Didn't you read the parts about how he called me Smella—a bunch of times, and then he called me Spilla, and then he called me Smella again?!"

"Yes," Mom said. "And Joshua was wrong to say those things. But you were wrong, too. When you told Joshua he was the reason you weren't going, that was wrong. It hurt his feelings."

"But he'd already hurt mine," I reminded her. "And that was wrong."

"Two wrongs don't make a right. You know that."

"I'm sorry," I said. "I was just so sad because . . . well, I do want to go see the show being taped."

"I told you that you would," Mom reminded me.

"How did you know that?"

"I've been your mom a long time," Mom told me, just like she'd told Penny yesterday. "And I've paid a lot of attention to the things you want to do. It was just a feeling I had."

"But I didn't even know I would feel that way!"

"It's all right," Mom said. "You're only eight, and you're going to get things wrong sometimes. But when you do, it's really important to apologize."

"I have to say sorry to Joshua?"

"You got it," Mom said.

"But he really is the biggest meanie in my whole entire class! I don't think anyone has ever had to apologize to him. He's always the one who has things to be sorry for."

"I know he's not the nicest to you. But in this case, can you look beyond the mean things and see some nice things he was doing?"

"Look beyond the mean things? Like when he called me Smella the first time, and the second, and the third, and the fourth, and then I spilled. And even when he brought the napkins and helped me—"

"Ah," Mom interrupted. "What was that you just said?"

"When he brought the napkins and helped me," I repeated. "He was the only one who was left, because everyone else ran out to the playground, and Miss Linka made him."

Mom shook the pages of my play in her hand. "And according to this very well-written script, Joshua stayed to help up until the moment you hurt his feelings, right?"

I nodded. "Yeah, he did," I admitted.

"When you hurt someone's feelings, you have to apologize. That's a Ground Rule in this family. I'm going to get the phone now, okay?"

"I have a better idea. I'll write a note and give it to him tomorrow."

Actually, maybe I shouldn't give it to him in person tomorrow—then people would see and know I'd done something wrong.

"Or better than that—I can mail it to him. Kids love mail way more than adults do."

"That's because all adults get are bills," Mom said.

"Or I could just think about apologizing to Joshua in my head," I said. "Because I really am sorry. I'm thinking about it right now. And it's the thought that counts, right?"

Mom shook her head. "I'll be right back with the phone. Then you can get it over with."

She came back in a couple minutes later. She had Joshua's number on our class phone list and she let me dial myself. But when it started to ring, I handed her the phone.

"This is your call, Stel."

"Can't you ask for Joshua? I don't want to

have to talk to his parents, too." (What if he told his mom and dad what I said?)

Mom took the phone back. I could hear through the receiver when someone answered, and Mom said, "Hi, Annette? This is Elaine Batts, Stella's mom." Pause. "Yes, we are all very excited about Penny's television debut. How's your family doing?" Another pause. "Glad to hear it," Mom said.

I guessed Mrs. Lewis didn't say anything bad about me, or Mom wouldn't have been glad about it.

"Well, Stella is actually calling for Joshua. Is he available?"

"Yes," I heard Mrs. Lewis say through the phone. I was scrunched up close enough to Mom to hear.

"Thanks, I'm going to hand the phone off, too," Mom said. She handed me the phone in time for me to hear Joshua shout to his mother. "Do I really have to talk to Smella Batts?"

And then there was a scratchy noise. I knew that meant Mrs. Lewis was covering the phone with her hand. A few seconds passed. I scrambled for a piece of paper and a pencil and wrote a note to Mom: I don't think Joshua wants to talk to me.

"Just leave a message with Mrs. Lewis," Mom whispered. "Tell her to tell Joshua you're sorry."

Oh, that would be so much worse! Having to tell a grown-up that you're sorry!

But then Joshua's voice came on the line. "Hi, Smella, why are you calling me?"

I heard Mrs. Lewis hiss something at him. "Fine. I meant *Stella*," he said.

I felt my heart beating fast, even though

it was just Joshua and not a grown-up. Still, his mom was listening to him—and I was sure he'd told her what I'd said. And my mom was still listening to me.

"Well?" Joshua asked.

I took a deep breath to get braver. Then I took another one.

"I can hear you breathing," Joshua said.

I took one last deep breath and let it out. "I'm sorry about what I said earlier," I said. "I didn't mean it when I said I wasn't going because I didn't want to be near you."

"I don't care," Joshua said. "Actually I'm really happy you won't be there!"

"Joshua!" I heard Mrs. Lewis say.

"I have to go," I told him.

"Bye, Smell—"

"Joshua!" Mrs. Lewis said again. "Didn't you tell me you didn't understand why Stella wouldn't want to be near you? Maybe it's time for us to have a long conversation about why."

There was a click then.

"Hello? Hello?" I asked. "He hung up without saying good-bye," I told Mom.

"You did the right thing," Mom said. "That's what matters the most."

Then how come it didn't feel like it mattered at all? My feelings were hurt, my best friend was going with my sister, and I wouldn't get to meet Superstar Sam at all! The Hot Tamales behind my eyes exploded and I started to cry.

CHAPTER 8

Things Couldn't Get Much Worse

Penny wasn't in carpool with us that morning. That's because she wasn't going to school. Because she was really nervous and wanted to practice her lines.

"Dawn got these jitters, too," Mom said. "Show business is not a good business for kids."

Now I actually agreed with her!

Evie was in carpool. "Let me see your note," I said.

She handed it over. It was in Mrs. King's loopy handwriting, in cursive.

Dear Mrs. Finkel,
Please excuse Evie from school today at twelve o'clock. She will be picked up by David Batts, Stella's father.
Thank you,
Julie King

It was weird that Evie was going to be picked up by my dad, and I would be staying behind at school. There should be a Ground Rule against that.

At snack time, Mrs. Finkel clapped her hands and Evie gathered up her stuff to leave for the day. "Bye, Evie!" everyone called. "Take lots of pictures!"

Pictures?! She'd get a picture with

Superstar Sam?!

"Take lots of notes," Lucy added. "That way you'll remember everything that happens."

Taking notes is like writing and that's usually MY job.

"Bye, Stella," Evie said.

"Bye," I said from over by my desk. We weren't all gathering by Evie's desk that day since she was leaving.

"Knock knock!" Talisa said.

"Who's there?"

"Us."

"Us who?"

"All of us at your desk!"

It was true. She was standing there with our other usual snack-time hang-out friends Lucy and Arielle . . . and Joshua?

Why was he always hanging around with

us? Especially if he hated me so much.

Sometimes I think of questions in my head but I don't ask them out loud because they're not very nice.

Except now Joshua and I had so many wrongs piled up, it's not like one more wrong could make any difference. Things couldn't get any worse!

"Why do you always hang out with us at snack time if you hate me so much?" I asked.

"Yeah," Lucy said. "Aren't you going to watch the show being made anyway? You said your uncle was the boss of it. Were you lying about that?"

"No!" he said. "Smell—I mean Stella—met my uncle! He really is the boss! And it's her fault I'm here and not there."

And with that he stomped his foot, and Mrs. Finkel had to call out, "Joshua, this may be the talking part of snack time, but outbursts are still not allowed. That's a Ground Rule."

"Besides it's not my fault," I said. "I'm not the boss of you."

If I were, I'd make up a whole lot more Ground Rules for Joshua. Starting with: Don't ever call me Smella again, not even the beginning syllable of calling me Smella, or else . . . or else . . .

"It is too your fault," he said. "After I got off the phone with you last night, my mom said I had been rude and she was taking away privileges—starting with the privilege of going to the show today. Which is fine with me, because *Superstar Sam*'s just a dumb show anyway, and—"

"Wait," I interrupted. "Are you saying now there's an extra seat at the filming?"

"Yes," Joshua said. "Actually three extras

because my cousin Bruce isn't going either. He has the flu. And my mom isn't going because she doesn't care so much about the show. And neither do I. Just like you, Stella."

He called me Stella!

But I *did* care. "Everything got a little mixed up," I said. "And Evie got my place. But I do want to go."

"If I apologize to you about yesterday, we could go together," Joshua said.

"What?"

"You apologized to me, and now I'm apologizing to you. Do you accept?"

"I do," I told him.

"You sound like you're getting married!" Lucy said.

"Ew," Talisa said.

"We're not getting married," I said. "This is way more important. So I accept and you accept, and now how do we get there? My dad already picked up Evie. And we don't have a car."

"And you can't even drive," Lucy pointed out.

"Right, so now what?"

"Mrs. Finkel!" Joshua shouted. "Mrs. Finkel, I need to call my mom!"

"That's outburst number two," Mrs. Finkel told him. "One more and you'll have to take a trip to Mr. O'Neil's office."

Then Mrs. Finkel started clapping her hands, which meant the talking part of snack time was over. My friends left the area by my desk and went to sit at theirs, pull out their snacks, and eat up before Mrs. Finkel clapped again and it was time to get back to our lessons.

"But," Joshua said, and Mrs. Finkel brought a finger to her lips and had a look in her eyes. A look that said: *I'm serious about sending you to the principal if there's any more disruptive behavior!*

But if we weren't allowed to talk, then Joshua couldn't explain why he had to call his mom.

"Excuse me, Mrs. Finkel?" I said.

"Yes, Stella?"

"I have to call my mom, too." If I called my mom, maybe she could call Joshua's mom and explain everything.

"Is it an emergency?"

"Um."

What's an emergency? Like if someone is super sick and needs to get to the hospital. Or if a cat is stuck in a tree. Or if someone goes into a pool without a grown-up nearby.

"Not exactly," I said. "But if we call then we can meet Superstar Sam."

"Ah yes," Mrs. Finkel said. "I've watched that show with my son. But that sounds like something that can wait until after school."

Which of course it couldn't! After school would be too late!

"But, Mrs. Finkel," I said.

"That's enough, Stella," Mrs. Finkel said. "I don't expect any more disruptive behavior out of you."

I lowered my head and stared at my desk. I wasn't hungry for the snack in my lunch box—NOT AT ALL. Even though it was fudge that Mom had packed special, to cheer me up.

Nothing was going to cheer me up on this day.

Suddenly there was a loud WHACK sound from behind me. I turned to look. Joshua had slammed his hand down on his desk, which is one of the things he does when

he's not getting his way. But this time he'd slammed it harder than ever before. "Ow ow ow ow OWWWWWWWWWWWWW!" he cried.

"Joshua Lewis!" Mrs. Finkel said. "Three strikes and you're out—to Mr. O'Neil's office."

"I think I need to see Nurse Tucker," he said, shaking out his hand. He was shaking it so hard it looked like he was hurting it even more.

"Good thing the nurse is next door to the principal," Mrs. Finkel said. She scribbled a note at her desk. "Clark, will you take this note, and take Joshua up to Mr. O'Neil's?"

I watched Joshua and Clark walk out of the room. Mrs. Finkel said, "Math books on your desks, please," and I swallowed the gobstopper that was in the back of my throat, and opened my book like I was supposed to.

A few minutes later Clark came back in— without Joshua. Mrs. Finkel kept going with our math lesson. We were doing comparison fractions. "What's larger?" she asked. "A half, or five-ninths?"

Some kids raised their hands—raised them quietly, because that's a Ground Rule. Joshua is the only one who raises his hand and waves it around, and says, "Ooh, ooh, ooh," when he wants Mrs. Finkel to pick him.

Which never works.

"Yes, Talisa?" Mrs. Finkel said.

CREAK went the door as it opened.

Of course then everyone in the whole entire class looked away from Mrs. Finkel, even Talisa. We all looked right at Joshua, who was walking back into the classroom. "I have a—" Joshua started to say, holding a note out in his hand.

By the way, his hand was wrapped in a bandage.

"Shh," Mrs. Finkel said. "I'll take the note, and you can return to your desk quietly."

Joshua walked to the front of the room. He handed the note to Mrs. Finkel. I could tell it was a different one from the one Mrs. Finkel had given him when he'd left. This one was on paper that was more like a card, like special stationery. Not just plain loose-leaf paper like Mrs. Finkel had used.

Mrs. Finkel turned to put the note down on her desk. "Talisa? You have an answer for us."

"Wait," Joshua said. "You have to read it right away. It's from Mr. O'Neil."

No wonder the stationery looked so special: It was PRINCIPAL stationery.

You could tell Mrs. Finkel didn't want to do something just because Joshua told her to.

But Mr. O'Neil is the principal, so he's the boss of everyone. If he wrote the note, Mrs. Finkel did have to read it right away. Joshua was right about that.

Mrs. Finkel unfolded the note.

Joshua looked over at me and smiled.

Pop Rocks started jumping around my stomach. I didn't want to get my hopes up. It hadn't worked out so well before.

But you can't help whether your hopes are up or down. They are like feelings. They just happen.

And this time my hopes were saying: Please, please, PLEASE LET THE NOTE FROM THE PRINCIPAL TELL MRS. FINKEL THAT JOSHUA AND I GET TO GO TO THE SUPERSTAR SAM FILMING!!!!!!!!!!

Mrs. Finkel was frowning but the

words that came out of her mouth were
actually all good.

She said, "Stella, it seems you and Joshua
are to pack up all of your belongings for the
day. Mrs. Lewis will be picking you both up."

CHAPTER 9

Take Ten

There was a sign on the door to Brody's Grill that said CLOSED.

But even though the door said closed, there were a lot of people outside wanting to get in. They couldn't, though, because a man with a clipboard was guarding the door.

Mrs. Lewis went right up to him. "We're here to watch them film the show," she said. "I'm Annette Lewis. I believe there are three seats inside reserved in my name."

The guard checked his clipboard. "Yes, yes. I see you here. But they're filming right now, so you're going to have to wait for a break."

Wow, filming had started already?!

We couldn't even look through the windows because they were blacked up like someone had put construction paper covering them up. All we could do was wait.

Waiting is one of my LEAST favorite things.

And one of Joshua's least favorite things, too. He didn't say so but I could tell because he kept pacing back and forth and kicking at invisible things on the sidewalk. Then Mrs. Lewis told him to cut it out, so he didn't hurt his foot on top of already hurting his hand.

"I just want to get in already," Joshua said. "Otherwise I hurt my hand for nothing."

"Don't think I've forgotten about that, Joshua," Mrs. Lewis said. "We're going to have a long talk about behavior when we get home later."

I could tell Joshua was embarrassed his mom said that in front of me because the tips of his ears turned red. I felt bad for him. But most of all I felt worried—worried that they wouldn't take any filming breaks and we'd miss the whole show!

About a hundred years later, there was a knock at the door.

Okay, fine, it wasn't a hundred years, but it felt like it.

It must've been some kind of signal, because the guard opened the door and we were allowed to walk inside.

"They're not done filming yet, are they?" I asked Mrs. Lewis.

"I'm sure they're not," she said. "Let's find your dad."

"Take ten, everyone," someone called.

Then Hal Lewis came over to say hello to us and take us to the area where we could watch everything.

"Did Penny finish yet?" I asked.

"Oh no," Hal Lewis said. "She's just taking

a ten-minute break. Come along."

We walked across the restaurant. It didn't actually look like a restaurant at all anymore. The tables that usually stood in the middle of the room had been cleared out. Instead, there was a bunch of huge black lights set up around the room, and guys holding cameras. There was also a big huge white sheet, and black wires that—

"Watch that!" Mrs. Lewis said.

—that crisscrossed the floor, so you had to watch where you were going and not trip over them. Which I almost did because I was busy looking at everything.

I couldn't help it! Everything was interesting!

Like the chairs. Not the regular restaurant chairs that were usually in the middle of the dining room. These were like fancy folding chairs. On the back SUPERSTAR SAM was written out in big block letters.

Wow! I wished I could have a chair like that! I'd get rid of my plain old desk chair and have an official

SUPERSTAR SAM chair!

"Stella!" Evie called. "You're here! I thought you weren't going to come."

"I'll tell you about it later," I told her. There were much more important things to discuss right then. "First you have to tell me everything we've missed. And where's Penny? And where's my dad? Isn't he supposed to be sitting with you?"

"He's backstage with Penny."

Backstage?! The restaurant had a backstage!!

"Because Penny was having a little problem."

"What problem?" Joshua asked.

"I don't really know what happened," Evie said. "I was standing here with your dad. Penny was over there." She pointed to a restaurant table lit up by a spotlight. "With

Superstar Sam and another actor."

"The one who played the waiter, I bet," I said.

"And when it was time for Penny, she didn't say it quite right. And that guy over there called, 'Cut!' "

"Is he the director?" I asked.

"Maybe," Evie said. "He said, 'Let's go again,' but Penny wouldn't go again. Then they called for a break, and then you guys came in."

"Was the director mad?" Joshua asked. "Did he yell at her?"

"Poor Penny!" I said. I wanted to be on a show, but not with a director who was a meanie.

"He didn't, don't worry," Evie said.

"Maybe we should get you backstage, Stella," Hal Lewis said. "Maybe what Penny needs right now is her older sister to give her a little confidence."

We went out the back door of Brody's Grill, and you know what was there? Big campers! Except they weren't for camping. They were for the actors and all the other TV people to get ready. Plus there was a table of food. Even though we were already right by A RESTAURANT. There was more food. It all looked super yummy. But there was no time to waste tasting it.

"This way," Hal Lewis said, taking me into one of the campers. Inside it was kind of like a hair-cutting place, because it had chairs set up in front of big mirrors. On the counter in front of the chairs there were all sorts of hair things, and makeup things.

And there was Dad and Penny.

And another lady.

And Superstar Sam.

Oh my goodness. There was Superstar Sam.

For real.

In my real life.

We were in the same room. (Well, in the same camper.) We were breathing the SAME AIR.

I felt my breath catch in my throat like a gobstopper.

Penny sniffled. Then Dad said, "Look, Penny! Your sister is here to see you!"

And Superstar Sam turned around to look at me.

That's right. Out of all the things she could look at, she decided to look at me.

"It's nice to meet you," she said. "I'm Thalia Lyn Blake."

CHAPTER 10

Small Enough, Big Enough

I know you're supposed to talk after someone introduces herself. You're supposed to say, "It's nice to meet you, too." Or something like that.

But my cheeks were burning hot as Red Hots candies, and it felt like there wasn't air left in my lungs and there wasn't spit left in my mouth. Even though I'd been waiting almost my whole entire life to meet Superstar Sam, when she was actually standing in the same room as me, I couldn't speak at all.

Then the other lady introduced herself. "I'm Oshyn," she said. "It's pronounced like 'ocean,' but spelled O-S-H-Y-N. A bit of creativity on my parents' part, don't you think?"

I knew what she doing. She was trying to distract me, the way Dad sometimes tried to distract Penny. In fact he did it when I walked in the room and he said, "Look, Penny! Your sister is here to see you!" Because she was crying, and he wanted to distract her.

But I couldn't be distracted.

I couldn't focus on Penny's crying.

And I couldn't focus on Oshyn explaining her name.

There was only one person I could focus on. I was staring at her. I knew it wasn't nice to stare, but I couldn't help myself.

"You're Stella, right?" I heard Superstar Sam say. She was speaking slowly, like she was afraid I wouldn't understand. "I've heard so much about you."

"You have?" I managed to choke out.

"Yeah, your sister was telling me all about you," she said.

"I was telling her that you were supposed to be the one in the show, not me!" Penny said. "Because I'm too little, like you said! I can't do it!"

"Of course you can do it," Dad told her. "You can do anything you want to do."

Penny covered her face with her hands. She was sniffling a lot. The worst part about crying is all the gross snot that comes along with it.

Superstar Sam plucked a couple tissues from a box on a shelf by the makeup mirror.

"Hey, Penny," she said. "I was just as scared as you, the first time I was on TV. It's perfectly normal. Don't you think, Stella?"

Oh my goodness! Superstar Sam was talking to me again!

"I've never been on TV," I admitted.

Which was sort of embarrassing since I was the older sister. I should've done things before Penny. Now my first conversation—probably my only conversation—with Superstar Sam was about the things I hadn't done.

I wanted to tell her I'd written seven books and I was working on my eighth! But it didn't seem like the right time, with Penny crying. Superstar Sam went on about how excited she was to work with Penny. I knew she was trying to make Penny feel better. But it actually sounded like she really meant it.

"You're so lucky," I told my sister. "Everybody wants to meet Superstar—I mean Thalia."

I always thought of her as Superstar Sam. It was hard to remember to use her real name.

"You're meeting her now, too," Penny pointed out. "And you don't have to be on TV."

"That's true," I said. "But if you're on

TV with her, everyone gets to see and that's way better. That means everyone will know you got to meet her. At least everyone who watches the show will know about it."

As I said it, I felt my own eyes tear up just an eensy weensy bit. I blinked them back. I didn't want to cry and have my own gross snot in front of Superstar Sam!

"Every kid in the whole entire world wants to do what you're getting to do right now," I told Penny.

"Every kid but me!" Penny said. "Stella, will you do it for me?"

What did she just say? She wanted ME to be on TV with Superstar Sam instead?

Oh my goodness! OH MY GOODNESS!!

"Do you mean it?" I asked. I'd pictured the whole thing in my head. And now I'd actually get to be in the scene with Superstar

Sam! And my name would be in the credits! And everyone would know!

"Yeah," Penny said.

"I guess it's a good thing I practiced with you so much yesterday!" I said. My voice came out kind of scream-y, because I was so excited. "I know all your lines! I know all of everyone's lines!"

"I don't think it works that way, girls," Dad said gently. "The casting director decides who gets to play the parts, not the kids."

"Actually," Hal Lewis said. "That's not a bad idea, having Stella substitute for Penny. Hang on."

He pulled a cell phone out of his pocket. I didn't know who he was calling, but I listened carefully to his end of the conversation. He explained the situation, and then there were lots of *mmmhmms* and *yups* and *you got its*.

He hung up the phone. "All right," he said.

"You mean I have the part?" I asked.

"Yup. Let's do this."

All of a sudden there was a burst of activity. Oshyn made Penny get up out of her chair and pulled me into it. She started powdering my face. You get to wear MAKEUP when you go on TV! I didn't know that!

"What about her clothes?" Hal Lewis asked.

"Penny will have to take off that outfit so we can try it out on Stella," Oshyn said.

"Will it fit her?" Hal Lewis asked.

"I'm not that much bigger," I told him. I never thought being the shortest one in my class would come in so handy, but it did!

"Why don't you go into the bathroom and change?" Oshyn asked Penny.

"All right, sweetheart?" Dad asked her.

Penny shook her head. "I wish I wasn't so scared," she said. "I wish I were as brave as Stella."

As brave as me?

But I wasn't feeling brave right then. I was feeling lucky. Lucky that Penny was scared.

And that made me feel kind of bad. Because I didn't want good things to happen to me just because they weren't happening to Penny.

I looked at her, standing next to Dad. She was looking at me like I was a superstar—an even more famous one than Superstar Sam.

"We really need those clothes," Oshyn said quietly.

"Go on back to the bathroom to change," Dad told Penny.

There was a bathroom in the trailer!

But there was no time to think about how

cool it was.

"Hold on," I told Oshyn. I started to stand up from the makeup chair. "I just need to speak to my sister for a couple minutes."

"Sorry, hon," she said, putting her hand on my shoulder. "We don't have much time."

"We don't have *any* time," Hal Lewis said. "We're already three minutes past the take ten."

"Just *one* more minute?" I asked. "Please?"

Oshyn looked over at Hal.

"Thirty seconds," he said.

I jumped off the chair and raced toward Penny. I pulled her into the bathroom, not because I wanted her to start changing. But because I wanted privacy for us. We were about to have a serious sisters conversation.

"You know how you like to copy me?" I asked her.

"And you hate it," Penny replied. Her voice still had a lot of sniffle and cry in it. It made me feel bad all over again, even though that wasn't what she was crying about.

"Sometimes," I admitted. "But imitation is the sincerest form of flattery. And you should copy me right now. I wouldn't mind at all. Be brave like me, and then you can be on the show."

"But, Stella, I don't know how."

"Well, you're lucky because I DO know how to be like me, and I can teach you."

"Stella!" Dad called. "They really need you out here RIGHT NOW. And they need you out of those clothes, Pen!"

"Come on," I said. "Come back into the makeup chair, and I'll give you tips while Oshyn fixes you all up."

Everyone was pretty surprised when we

came out of the bathroom and told them the plan. But since there wasn't much time, they didn't argue. Oshyn got to work, and I gave Penny my tips.

"You should stretch before you go out, by putting your arms up like this and cracking your knuckles." I demonstrated for her. "And you should think about the delicious treat of fudge you'll get to eat when it's all over." I turned to Dad. "We can have treats after, right?"

"Oh yes," Dad said. "Treats for everyone."

"I love fudge!" Superstar Sam said.

"Me too," I said. Whoa, I had something in common with Superstar Sam!

"And what else?" Penny asked.

Oh, right. Back to the advice. I had to lean in toward her ear to tell her the next one. "When you need an extra eensy weensy bit of

luck, click your heels together three times."

I'd never told anyone else that last piece of advice. It was the secret thing I did. But Penny needed to know, and I trusted her not to tell anyone else.

Oshyn finished Penny's makeup. Then she touched up Superstar Sam's a little bit.

Even though if you asked me, she already looked perfect. Then Hal Lewis scooted the two of them out of the trailer.

Dad and I followed behind, and went back into Brody's Grill where the non-actors were standing.

"What took you so long, Smell—I mean Stella?" Joshua asked.

"Is Penny all right?" Evie asked.

I looked across at Penny. She was sitting at the table with Superstar Sam, and she was stretching her arms up to crack her knuckles. I bet under the table, she was clicking her heels together, too. "Everything's fine," I said.

Then the director-guy called, "Lock it up!"

"That means everyone is in their places," Evie whispered to me. "Hal Lewis told me that the first time they tried to do this scene.

But then Penny started to cry."

"Quiet on the set!" someone else called.

"Rolling!"

"And action!"

It was funny to hear Superstar Sam, and Penny, and the other actors say out loud the same lines I'd read when I'd practiced with Penny the day before. Nobody made any mistakes. Not even Penny.

"Cut! Let's go again!" the director called when it was all done.

I don't know why they had to do it again when no one had made a mistake. I could tell, because I knew the script by heart. But they did it again, and again after that.

"Cut!" he called.

Superstar Sam got up to stretch. Penny did, too.

"Something's not working," he said. "I

think we need to get more of a restaurant vibe going. Maybe another table in here. Do we have any extras?"

Extra tables?

Of course there were extra tables. This was a restaurant!

"We can drum some up," Hal Lewis said. "How many are you looking for?"

"Three or four at a table," the director said. "You know, a family."

Oh, he meant extra *people*.

"I'll take care of it," Hal said.

A bunch of people got up and started moving a table and chairs into place right next to where Penny and Superstar Sam's table was. But Hal walked away from the set and toward the crowd where the rest of us were standing around watching all the action.

Can you guess what happened next?

If you said that Hal Lewis picked ME to be one of the extras, then you are absolutely right!

Actually, he picked me, and Joshua, and Joshua's mom, and my dad. And then he picked Evie too, so she wouldn't be left out.

They set up a table with five chairs around it, and we had to pretend to be eating and talking to each other, but actually we weren't really, because if we really talked it might be too loud and mess up the conversation they were really trying to film. They told us to just mouth the word "watermelon" over and over again, because it doesn't look like you're saying watermelon. It just looks like you're talking. Isn't that a cool TV trick?!

Watermelon, watermelon, watermelon, we all mouthed. The other actors—including Penny!—said their lines out loud.

"Cut!"

"Let's go again!"

"Cut!"

"Let's go again!"

We had to go again like another ten times.

Here's something I learned about being in a TV show. Even though it is very very VERY cool to know you're being filmed in something that will be on TV for everyone to see, the actual filming part is an eensy weensy bit boring.

And then finally the director said the three very best words: "That's a wrap!"

CHAPTER 11

Wrap Party

After about a dozen takes, with breaks for Oshyn to run in and fix people's hair or powder their faces, it was all over.

"Penny, you were so good!" I said, now that I was allowed to actually speak out loud and not just pretend to be talking.

"I knew you could do it," Dad said.

Superstar Sam gave her a hug, and then she gave ME a hug. "Thanks for all your help," she told me.

I felt an eensy weensy bit speechless again, and I said, "You're welcome," in my softest voice.

There were more hugs, and lots of action going on—not the filming kind of action. Just the activity kind, of people moving around, talking, that kind of thing. We were scooted off to the side so we wouldn't get in anyone's way.

And there was someone waiting for us. "Mom! You're here! But I thought . . . what are you doing here?"

"I snuck in at the last minute," she explained. "I didn't want to miss my girls' television debut—especially since it's not going to happen again for a long time."

"Until we're grown-ups," Penny said.

"And maybe not even then," I added. "I don't know if I want to be an actress anymore.

I think I'm happy just being a writer."

"Whatever you want to be is fine with me," Mom said. "But you have plenty of time to decide. You get to be a kid first."

"Do we still have time for treats?" I asked Dad.

"Oh yeah!" Joshua said. "TREATS!"

He doesn't even use his inside voice on a TV set.

Dad looked at his watch. "We've got to get home for your brother."

"Why don't you get Marco," Mom said. "I'll take our TV stars for a treat."

"Goody!" I said.

"Are you getting fudge?" Superstar Sam asked.

Oh my goodness, I didn't realize she was standing right behind me! And now she was talking to me again! This was our THIRD conversation!

I wished I hadn't said "goody" in front of her, since that was kind of babyish. I felt my cheeks warm up, and I knew they were getting that pink bubble gum-ish color they get when I'm a little embarrassed. "Yeah," I said. "That's what I always get when we go to Batts Confections."

"It's our store," Penny added.

"You have a candy store?!" Superstar Sam asked.

"Yup," Penny said.

"That's the coolest thing I've ever heard!"

"But you're on TV!" I said. "What could be cooler than that?"

"Owning my very own candy store."

"It's not really our very own," I said. "Our parents are the owners."

"It's still super cool."

"Do you want to come?" I asked.

"Sure," she said. Oh my goodness! Superstar Sam was going to come to OUR store?! "Let me ask my mom."

Superstar Sam had a mom! A real-live one, not the one who was her mom on TV.

I mean, of course she did. But I guess I kind of forgot that she was a regular person, too.

Maybe it was time I started thinking about her as Thalia.

"Hey, Mom!" she called out. A woman who'd been standing in the background the whole time turned around. I had no idea she was Thalia's mom. Boy, she must be so proud of her daughter. Like, the proudest mom in the whole entire world.

"Yes?" she said.

Superstar Sam—I mean Thalia—

explained the situation, and her mom said yes, of course she could come. She introduced herself to my mom. Wouldn't it be amazing if they turned into friends? Then we could all hang out all the time, or at least whenever Thalia had to film things in Somers!

We walked out the door to head down the sidewalk to Batts Confections. There were tons of people on the sidewalk who knew about the show being filmed, and wanted to have their pictures taken with Thalia, and get her autograph. She smiled for every picture, and signed every piece of paper that people held out to her.

Finally we made it into the door of Batts Confections. Stuart was working at the store. So were Jess and Claire. It was pretty crowded since now it was Friday afternoon, school was out, and lots of kids love our store. It seemed

like everyone there wanted to meet Thalia, too. Mom suggested Thalia and her mom go downstairs, to Mom and Dad's office, so they could get away from the crowd. "Penny, why don't you show them the way? And give us your candy order. We'll meet you down there."

Joshua was ticking off just about every item we have in the store for his order, plus a milkshake to wash it all down. But then his mom said he could get one thing, that was it.

"Aw, man!" he said.

"We have coffee, if you want," I told Thalia. "I know that's what teenagers like. Sometimes I like it, too."

"Stella!" Mom said. "No coffee."

"Do you have hot chocolate?" Thalia asked.

"Yes," Penny said. "We have the best kind—with whipped cream on top, and caramel mixed in."

"Can I have some of that, please?" Thalia asked. "I don't really like coffee, but I love hot chocolate. And if I'm allowed a second thing, I'd love to try the fudge."

"What flavor?"

"There's more than one flavor?"

"Lots more," I told her. "We can bring

slivers of a bunch, right, Mom?"

Slivers are eensy sample-sized pieces, so you can taste more than one flavor.

"Of course," Mom said.

We got hot chocolate and slivers of fudge in every flavor. (And actually Stuart had cut us the biggest slivers I'd ever seen. They were almost the size of real pieces.) Mom and I brought it all downstairs.

I took the elevator with all the stuff, and Mom took the stairs. She met me at the elevator door and helped me carry it all into the office.

"It's a wrap party!" Thalia Lyn Blake said. Which is the kind of party you have when you're all done with filming.

I learned that from Thalia. I also learned some other things about her, like:

1. The first acting job she ever had was

being a baby in a diaper commercial.

2. She doesn't want to be an actress when she grows up. She wants to be a scientist.

3. She has two best friends named Wren and Charlie.

"I have two best friends, too," I said.

"Evie and Joshua," Thalia guessed.

"Ew, no!" Joshua said.

"Evie and Willa," I said. "Willa moved to Pennsylvania, so I don't get to see her every day anymore."

"I don't get to see my best friends every day either," Thalia said.

Another thing we had in common!

I reached for a piece of peanut butter-butterscotch fudge. "Hey, that's the one I was going to pick," Joshua said. "Can we split it?"

"You can have the whole thing," I told him. After all, if it wasn't for Joshua, I wouldn't have been able to go to the filming. Then I wouldn't have been there to help Penny, or to be an extra, or to invite Thalia to Batts Confections for candy and hot chocolate. I owed him a lot, and I think that made us friends. Even if we still weren't best ones.

I cut in half the piece of Oreo chocolate fudge, which was one of my favorites anyway. "Anyone want the other half?" I asked.

"Me!" Penny said. I slid half over to her, and she dunked it in her hot chocolate and took a bite, chewed, and swallowed. "The best way to eat fudge is to dip it in hot chocolate because it gets melty and even more delicious!"

We all dipped fudge into our hot chocolate, took bites, and agreed with Penny.

"I know you signed lots of autographs," Evie said to Thalia. "But would you mind signing a few more? I promised my friends at school."

"Sure," Thalia said.

"Can I have your autograph, too?" Joshua asked.

I pulled my notebook out of my backpack and ripped out a few sheets of paper from the back. Evie told Thalia the names of our friends. Then Joshua handed over his piece of paper and said, "Can you sign it to Mrs. Finkel's son?"

"Mrs. Finkel's son?" Thalia asked.

"Yeah. Mrs. Finkel is my teacher, and her son likes your show. I think maybe if you signed something for him, she won't be mad at me tomorrow."

"Do you know her son's name?" Thalia asked.

"No," Joshua said.

"I do," I said. "His name is Evan."

I looked over as Thalia wrote:

Dear Evan,
Your mom has a very cool student named Joshua. He wanted me to sign this for you.
Best wishes, Thalia Lyn Blake

"Look, Mom!" Joshua said, holding it up. "It's for Mrs. Finkel's son! She said he likes this show!"

"That's a good start," she told him. "You can write an apology to Mrs. Finkel herself, and deliver them both tomorrow."

"I hate apologizing," Joshua said.

"Me too," I said. "But then sometimes the best things happen when you do. Like right now. This day is one of the very best days ever. I think I'm going to write it into my book. It can be the last chapter, because I always like to end my books on something really good that happens."

"You write books?" Thalia asked. Her eyes were suddenly open really wide, like she could hardly believe it.

"Yeah," I said. I tried to make my voice sound like it was no big deal, but I was starting to smile. "That's why I always have paper—because I take my notebook with me wherever I go, in case I think of things to write about. Like the line about tomatoes being a fruit, not a vegetable—I'm the one who told the casting people that!"

"Holy cow!" she said. "That was my favorite line! I can't believe you came up with it."

"I can't believe you're on TV," I told her. "But different people have different talents."

Just like my dad had said.

"Everyone has something that makes them special," I added.

Right then, I was so happy with what made me special. I was happy to be Stella.

Courtney Sheinmel

Courtney Sheinmel is the author of several books for middle-grade readers, including *Sincerely* and *All the Things You Are*. Like Stella Batts, she was born in California and has a younger sister, but unlike Stella, her parents never owned a candy store. Courtney now lives in New York City. Visit her online at www.courtneysheinmel. com where you can find out more about all the Stella Batts books.

Jennifer A. Bell

Jennifer A. Bell is an illustrator whose work can be found on greeting cards, in magazines, and in more than a dozen children's books. She lives in Minneapolis, Minnesota, with her husband and son. Visit her online at www.JenniferABell.com.

Praise for Stella Batts

"Sheinmel has a great ear for the dialogue and concerns of eight-year-old girls. Bell's artwork is breezy and light, reflecting the overall tone of the book. This would be a good choice for fans of Barbara Park's 'Junie B. Jones' books."

— *School Library Journal*

"First in a series featuring eight-year-old Stella, Sheinmel's unassuming story, cheerily illustrated by Bell, is a reliable read for those first encountering chapter books. With a light touch, Sheinmel persuasively conveys elementary school dynamics; readers may recognize some of their own inflated reactions to small mortifications in likeable Stella, while descriptions of unique candy confections are mouth-watering."

— *Publishers Weekly*

"Why five stars? Because any book that can make a reader out of a child deserves five stars in my book! It's all about getting kids 'hooked' on reading."

— Pam Kramer, Examiner.com

"My daughter is nine years old and struggled with reading since kindergarten. Recently we found the Stella Batts books and she has fallen in love with them. She has proudly read them all and she can't wait till #6. We can't thank you enough. Her confidence with reading has improved 100%. It brings tears to my eyes to see her excited about reading. Thanks."

— K.M. Anchorage, Alaska

Other books in this series:

★Stella Batts Needs A New Name

★Stella Batts Hair Today, Gone
  Tomorrow

★Stella Batts Pardon Me

★Stella Batts A Case of the Meanies

★Stella Batts Who's in Charge?

★Stella Batts Something Blue

★Stella Batts None of Your Beeswax

Stella Batts
Needs a New Name

Courtney Sheinmel
1
Illustrated by Jennifer A. Bell

Stella Batts
Hair Today, Gone Tomorrow

Courtney Sheinmel
2
Illustrated by Jennifer A. Bell

Stella Batts
Pardon Me

Courtney Sheinmel
3
Illustrated by Jennifer A. Bell

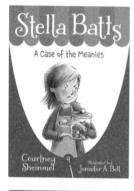

Stella Batts
A Case of the Meanies

Courtney Sheinmel
4
Illustrated by Jennifer A. Bell

Stella Batts
Who's in Charge?

Courtney Sheinmel
5
Illustrated by Jennifer A. Bell

Stella Batts
Something Blue

Courtney Sheinmel
6
Illustrated by Jennifer A. Bell

Stella Batts
None of Your Beeswax

Courtney Sheinmel
7
Illustrated by Jennifer A. Bell

Meet Stella and friends online
at www.stellabatts.com